Bookmarks Are People Too!

Henry Winkler & Lin Oliver

Illustrated by Scott Garrett

WALKER
BOOKS

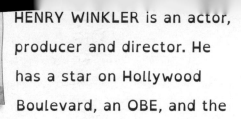

HENRY WINKLER is an actor, producer and director. He has a star on Hollywood Boulevard, an OBE, and the jacket he wore as the Fonz hangs in the Smithsonian Museum in Washington DC. But if you asked him what he's most proud of, he would say, "Writing the Hank Zipzer books with my partner, Lin Oliver." He lives in Los Angeles with his wife, Stacey.

LIN OLIVER is a writer and producer of films, books and television series for children and families. She is also co-founder and executive director of the Society of Children's Book Writers and Illustrators. She lives in Los Angeles with her husband, Alan.

who learns differently. To Stacey always

*For Leo Pasquale Confalone,
darling SCBWI poster boy! – L.O.*

For my beautiful boys, Texas & Tennessee – S.G.

First published in Great Britain 2015 by Walker Books Ltd
87 Vauxhall Walk, London SE11 5HJ

First published in the United States as *Here's Hank #1:
Bookmarks Are People Too!* (2014) by Henry Winkler and Lin Oliver.
Published by arrangement with Grosset & Dunlap™, an imprint of
Penguin Young Readers Group, a division of Penguin Random House LLC.
All rights reserved.

2 4 6 8 10 9 7 5 3 1

Text © 2014 Henry Winkler and Lin Oliver Productions, Inc.
Illustrations © 2014 Scott Garrett
Author photographs on page 1 by Jesse Grant/JPI and Sonya Sones

This book has been typeset in OpenDyslexic

Printed and bound in Great Britain by Clays Ltd, St Ives plc

British Library Cataloguing in Publication Data:
a catalogue record for this book is available from the British Library

ISBN 978-1-4063-6137-7

www.walker.co.uk

CHAPTER 1

"Hank Zipzer! Please stop talking!" Ms Flowers said to me. "Good citizens don't talk when the teacher is talking."

"But I didn't say anything, Ms Flowers."

"Hank, I saw your lips moving with my own two eyes."

"But no sound came out, Ms Flowers. So, technically, I wasn't talking."

"Then what exactly were you doing?"

"I was sending a signal."

The other kids in the class laughed, which made me feel great. I wasn't trying to be funny. But it's always nice to get a laugh.

My grandfather Papa Pete always says laughter is good, but not as good as a pickle. We're both big pickle fans.

"And to whom was this so-called signal being sent?" Ms Flowers asked.

"To me!" Frankie Townsend called out.

Frankie and I have been best friends since we were babies. We have a whole system of signals.

"We can talk without saying a word," I told Ms Flowers.

"Oh, really?" she said. "That's very unusual."

"There was this one time in the Museum of Natural History," Frankie went on. "It was amazing. Hank and I both decided to roar right in the T. rex's face — at the very same moment."

"It was awesome," I added. "Until the security guard told us there was no roaring allowed in the museum."

I laughed, and everyone joined in. Ms Flowers chuckled too. She's really nice about laughing. Everyone at PS 87 wants her for second grade because she's in a good mood almost all the time. She even gave me a NICE TRY when I only got two out of ten right on my spelling test last week.

"Well, Hank, since you're so expert at roaring and signalling," she said to me, "you're going to love our next class project."

"I can hardly wait to hear what it is. I'm sitting on the edge of my seat."

"I can hardly wait for you to fall off!" Nick McKelty shouted from the desk behind me.

Nick McKelty, better known as Nick the Tick, never has a nice word to say about anyone.

But he gets away with it because he's about twelve feet tall — in every direction.

"That's enough, Nick," Ms Flowers snapped, putting her hands on her hips. But McKelty didn't seem to care that she was angry. He just went back to what he always does — rolling spitballs to launch at the little kids during breaktime.

"Next week is Children's Reading Week," Ms Flowers went on. "We will be celebrating by

putting on a play. I wrote it myself. It's called *A Night at the Library.*"

Katie Sperling put up her hand and waved it around. "Can I be the star?" she asked. "My daddy always tells me I am one, anyway."

"Everyone will have a part," Ms Flowers said.

"Even me?" Luke Whitman asked, with his finger up his nose.

"Yes, even you, Luke."

I wondered if there was a part in the play for a champion nose-picker.

Luke Whitman would get that for sure!

"I think we all know who's going to be the star!" McKelty shouted out. "The one with the most talent. And that would be me."

Then, for no reason at all, he stood up and bowed, and let out one of his snorty laughs. No one else joined in.

"I'm now going to pass out the script," Ms Flowers said, motioning for McKelty to sit down. "Read the play over the weekend and decide which part you'd like."

I felt worried. Really worried. Normal second-grade reading is hard for me. Reading a whole script would be nearly impossible.

Frankie saw my face and sent me our "don't worry" signal. I relaxed right away, because I knew he would help me. Frankie is an excellent reader. Over the Christmas holidays, he read a two-hundred-page book that didn't even have pictures.

"We will hold auditions on Monday," Ms Flowers told us. "That's when you can each try out for the part you want."

Even though I knew Frankie would help me, I was starting to get very nervous.

"You'll have to learn your lines and be very prepared," Ms Flowers continued. "Does anyone have any questions?"

As usual, I had *many* questions. Also as usual, I was too embarrassed to ask them. So I did what I usually did — I made a list in my head.

CHAPTER 2

QUESTIONS I HAVE ABOUT THE PLAY (THAT I'M TOO AFRAID TO ASK)

BY HANK ZIPZER

1. Will I be any good at this?
2. I mean, will I *really* be any good at this?
3. What if I'm not good at this?
4. Can you throw up during an audition and still get the part?
5. And the big question: Will I be any good at this? Oh, I already said that.

CHAPTER 3

After school that day, Papa
Pete picked up Frankie and
me. Frankie's mum is a yoga
instructor, and she teaches
every Friday afternoon. She
is so good at yoga that she
can lift her foot off the floor
and squeeze her nose with her
toes like they're a swimmer's
clip.

While Frankie's mum's teaching,
Papa Pete takes Frankie and me
to the Crunchy Pickle. That's

the deli on 77th Street and Broadway that Papa Pete used to own. Now my mum is taking it over and trying to turn it into a healthy sandwich shop.

That is very bad news for salami.

As we walked towards the Crunchy Pickle, Frankie and I couldn't stop talking about the play. Actually, I did all the talking, and Frankie did all the listening.

"I was in a play once when I was your age," Papa Pete said when I finally took a breath.

"Were you the star?" I asked him.

"Not exactly. I played a tube

of toothpaste, but it was a very important tube. Harold Dunski was the star. He was lucky enough to get the part of Mr Toothbrush."

"What's so lucky about that?" I asked.

"Are you kidding, Hankie?" Papa Pete said. "Harold got to sing the big opening number. It was called 'Don't Forget to Flush and Brush'. The girls went crazy. In fact, years later he married the girl who played the sink."

"No offence, Papa Pete," Frankie said, "but this is kind of a disgusting story."

"Well, I'm just pointing out

that being in a play is a lot
of fun, but it's also a lot of
work. You have rehearsals to
go to, lines to memorize..."

"That's the part that scares
me the most," I said. "I'm pretty
bad at memorizing. I can't
even remember how to spell
neighbour."

"Don't be so hard on yourself,
Hankie," Papa Pete said. "You're
clever. You'll figure it out."

I wasn't so sure he was right
about that.

We had reached the entrance
to the Crunchy Pickle. Papa
Pete pulled open the glass
door. Frankie and I dashed
to the counter that held the

black-and-white biscuits.
They've been our favourite
ever since I can remember.
Just before we grabbed two,
my mum came out from the
back room.

"Whoa there, mister," she said.
"No biscuits until you've had a
healthy snack. I have some fresh
soylami right here."

My mum is trying to bring
luncheon meats into the
twenty-first century. She
makes everything out of soy.
Soylami, which tastes nothing
like salami. Soystrami, which
makes your tongue want to
go home without eating. And
the worst is soyloney, which

doesn't even *look* like baloney.
In fact, it's yellow.

"Mum!" I protested. "Frankie
and I have a lot of work to do,
and we need real brain food."

"Look at your sister," she
answered. "See how nicely
she's sitting in that front booth
enjoying her soy-meat platter?"

My sister, Emily, who is in the

first grade, does everything
perfectly. It's just like her to
enjoy fake meat. She also likes
doing her homework, reading
about lizards, clipping her
toenails and getting
all *As*. She is so
annoying.

"Why don't
you boys find
a seat," Papa
Pete said.
"I'll make you
a real sandwich,
with some pickles
on the side."

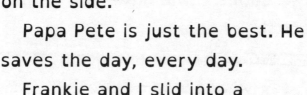

Papa Pete is just the best. He
saves the day, every day.

Frankie and I slid into a

booth far away from Emily. We reached into our backpacks and each pulled out a copy of the play. As soon as I turned to the first page, my brain froze like a Popsicle.

"I can't read this," I said to Frankie. "It's too many words."

"Yes, you can, Hank. Let's go very slowly."

Frankie read the summary of the story.

"It's about a boy named Barry who falls asleep in the library," he explained. "While he's asleep, the books come alive and jump off the shelves."

"Wow, that sounds great. Does it say what kinds of books?"

Frankie nodded. "The books
are all the characters the class
is going to play. Look, there's
a book on volcanoes."

"That'd be great for Luke
Whitman," I said. "His nose is
always full of lava." We cracked
up, and Frankie went on.

"Let's see. There's a biography of Martin Luther King Junior. And a mystery story called *The Secret of Big Bear Lake*. Here's a scary one called *My Babysitter Is a Zombie*. And look at this weird one — *The History of Shoes Up to the Flip-Flop*. You interested in that part?"

"No," I said, shaking my head. "I can't stand anything between my toes."

"Oh, this book is cool," Frankie said, pointing to some words on the page. "It's a superhero comic book called *Aqua Fly*. It's about a fly that lives in an underwater cave."

"That's perfect for me!"
I said. "I'm going for that part.
What about you, Frankie?"

"I think I'd be good at playing
Barry. I like to read in the
library. And I'm really good at
falling asleep."

"Great, then we both know
what we want," I said. "Let's
get to work."

I flipped through my script.
All the words started to swim
on the pages. I was hoping
that Aqua Fly didn't have too
many words to say. Maybe he
would just fly and buzz. I could
buzz for thirty-seven minutes
straight if I had to.

Unfortunately, Aqua Fly was

pretty talkative. As I tried to read all his lines, I could feel my brain start to swirl. After a few more pages, it felt like all I had in my head was soggy oatmeal.

"Here are your sandwiches, boys," Papa Pete said, sliding our plates onto the table next to the scripts.

Boy, oh, boy. I was never so glad to see a turkey sandwich and a pickle. They didn't have to read me, and I didn't have to read them. All I had to do was eat. And I am a champion eater.

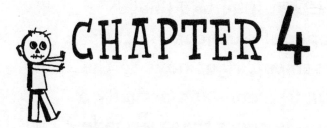# CHAPTER 4

Frankie and I stayed at the Crunchy Pickle for over an hour, eating our sandwiches and working on our lines.

As more customers came in, my mum said she needed the booth. So I kissed her goodbye, and Papa Pete took Frankie and me and, I'm sorry to say, Emily back to our apartment building.

Frankie lives on the fourth floor, and my family lives on

the tenth. He and I have a special clubhouse in the basement, right next to the laundry room. It's actually a storage room that we made into our clubhouse. We hang out there because it's really fun. Also, the air smells like soapsuds, which is very refreshing for my nose.

When we got home, we tried to continue our work on my dining-room table. My dad even moved his computer down to one end to make room for us. Also, he put on shoes so we didn't have to look at his toenails.

As Frankie and I started

going over the lines, my dad
looked up from his computer
screen.

"That doesn't sound like school work to me," he said.

"We're getting ready to audition for our class play," Frankie explained.

"Hank, you should be working on your writing and arithmetic skills," my dad said. "No one ever did well on a test by being in a play."

"This play is going to be really fun, Dad," I said. "And very educational, too."

"Oh, really?" my dad snapped. "Well then, how much is forty minus eighteen?"

I looked in every corner of my mind for the answer. It was nowhere to be found.

My brain can hear numbers, but it has no idea what to do with them. I mean, addition is hard. But subtraction is out of the question.

"I'll get back to you with the answer, Dad," I said. "In about five years."

"Trust me, Hank, it won't be that long," he said. "After dinner, I'm getting out the flash cards. It's going to be an all-subtraction evening."

What a horrible thought. Then, even more horribly, Emily

decided to take her baby pet
iguana, Katherine, on a walk
around the apartment. Every
time they passed, Katherine
shot her tongue out and tried
to touch my knuckles. Once,
she actually did. And let me
tell you, iguana tongue is very
sticky and rough.

"OK," I announced. "That does it for me. It's clubhouse time."

"You don't have to leave," Emily said. "Katherine enjoys the company."

"Oh, really? Then why is she hissing at us like a fire-breathing dragon?" Frankie asked.

"That's her way of saying *give me a hug*."

"Well, tell her my body is a hug-free zone," I answered. "Especially when it comes to lizards."

"She's an *iguana*, Hank."

"Whatever she is, she's ugly."

With that, a super-loud hiss flew out of Katherine's throat.

Frankie and I dashed out of the apartment and into the lift. Forty-two seconds later, we were in our clubhouse in the basement.

But there was already someone there!

As we rushed in, we saw a woman in a flowery dress standing on a ladder. Holding the ladder steady was a girl about our age. *A girl in our clubhouse? No, that's not in the rule book.*

"Hi," the girl said, turning to us. "I'm Ashley Wong. I just moved into the building, and I'm starting second grade on Monday at PS Eighty-Seven."

"We're second-graders too," Frankie said.

"Look at that! We've almost got a whole class in here," I added.

Ashley cracked up at that. "You're funny," she said.

"Hank's a riot," Frankie said. "He keeps everyone laughing. We call it the Zipzer attitude."

"Are you looking for something, Mrs Wong?" I asked the woman in the flowery dress who I guessed was Ashley's mother. "Frankie and I know everything in here."

"Mrs Park keeps her dog's raincoats in the box in the corner," Frankie said.

"And Mrs Fink keeps her gently used dressing-gowns in that big plastic container," I added. "Watch out if you go in there, though. You don't want to be digging around and suddenly find a set of her false teeth."

Ashley covered her mouth to hold in a laugh.

"We were putting away some boxes," Mrs Wong said, climbing down from the ladder. "Our family just moved into an apartment on the seventh floor and there isn't much cupboard space. We're finished now."

"Mum, can I stay down here with these guys?" Ashley asked.

"Of course, honey, if it's all

right with them. Just be back by dinner time. Your grandmother is making wonton soup."

"So, what do you want to do?" Ashley asked us.

Frankie and I just stood there with our mouths hanging open. This was *our* clubhouse. No girls allowed.

"Uh, actually, we have a lot of work to do down here," I said, trying to be polite. "We have to memorize lines for Ms Flowers's class play. Auditions are on Monday."

"Ms Flowers!" Ashley exclaimed. "She's going to be my teacher too. If I learn the play now, think what a great head start I'll have. This is just *so* perfect!"

Without waiting to be asked, she flopped down on the old flowery couch. The one that Frankie and I always sit on.

"Do you guys have the play?" she asked as her mum left. Then she noticed it lying on one of the cardboard boxes. She picked it up and starting flipping through the pages.

"Which part do you want, Hank?"

"Aqua Fly," I muttered. "I'm an excellent buzzer."

Ashley pushed her purple glasses back on her nose and laughed.

"You are such a crack-up," she said, holding up her hand for a high-five.

"Thanks," I said. I have to admit, I was beginning to like Ashley, even if she was a girl.

"Check it out, guys," Ashley said, continuing to turn the pages. Unlike me, she seemed to be able to read at lightning speed. "This part is totally me — the zombie from *My Babysitter Is a Zombie*. I have a great zombie walk."

She jumped to her feet and held her arms out in front of

her body. Then she staggered
around the clubhouse, bumping
into dusty boxes, old lamps and
piles of clothes. Each time she
hit something, she let out a long
moan. All of a sudden, she turned
to Frankie and me and pulled
down on her eyes so you could
see the icky red part inside.

"Zombie attack!" she screeched, lunging forwards until she fell on the couch in a heap, laughing her head off. Frankie and I held our sides and howled too.

And just like that, Ashley Wong became one of us.

CHAPTER 5

The three of us spent all weekend working on the play. Sometimes we were each in our own apartments. Sometimes we met in the clubhouse.

Of course, we took breaks. On Saturday, we went to Riverside Park for a snowball fight. Unfortunately, we ran into Nick the Tick McKelty there. When Frankie and I introduced him to Ashley, the first thing he did was make fun of her purple glasses.

Right away, McKelty found
out that wasn't such a great
idea when she whacked him
on the nose with a snowball.
It turns out Ashley Wong has
the arm of a shortstop.

"Hey!" McKelty yelled,
a clump of snow sliding down
into his mouth. "Nobody messes
with me."

"I just did," Ashley said. "You can make fun of my glasses all you want. But they helped me see well enough to hit you smack in the nose."

That shut him up. But Ashley wasn't finished.

"And as you can see," she added, "there is plenty more snow left."

McKelty had no comeback to that. He just ran off whimpering like a hurt puppy.

On Monday morning, my mum walked Frankie, Emily and me to school. As we left the apartment, we ran into Ashley and her mum, who were on their way to school too.

"Hello, I'm Dr Wong," Ashley's mother said, extending her hand to my mum.

"So nice to meet you," my mum answered. "I'm Randi Zipzer. Silly me. When I saw

Dr Wong written on your post box, I thought it was your husband."

"He *is* Dr Wong. And so am I."

"So your parents are Dr Wong and Dr Wong?" Emily asked.

"Exactly," Ashley said. "And they want me to be a doctor when I grow up too. Then we'll be Dr Wong, Dr Wong and Dr Wong. But I think that's just wrong."

Frankie and I cracked up.

As we all headed up 78th Street towards Amsterdam Avenue, Ashley asked Frankie if he was ready for the audition.

"Sure," he said. "I have my script right here in my backpack with my lines highlighted in yellow."

Script! Did he say script? Oh no. Where was *my* script? Suddenly, I couldn't remember where I'd put it. Was it in my backpack? Or did I leave it on the breakfast table next to the cereal box? I closed my eyes and tried to remember. As usual, my brain came up blank.

"Hold it, everyone," I said. "Stop right where you are."

I spun around so my back was facing Frankie.

"Unzip my backpack," I asked him. "And please tell me my script is in there."

I could feel Frankie tugging on the zip. Then I could feel his hand rummaging around inside.

"Is it there?" I asked.

"Give me a minute, Hankster. I'm still digging my way through the biscuit crumbs and bubble-gum wrappers. Don't you ever clean this thing out?"

"This is not the time to talk about neatness, Frankie."

"But it is the time to tell you that there is no script in here."

"You forgot it?" Emily, the Perfect One, said. "Honestly, Hank, we should put a Post-it note on your forehead."

"I have to go back and get it," I said.

"There isn't time, Hank," my mum said, checking her watch.

"Yeah," Emily piped up. "Just because the only thing you remember to pack are biscuit crumbs, doesn't mean *I* have to be late for school."

"Emily, did anyone ever tell you your braids are too tight?" I snapped.

"Don't worry about it, dude," Frankie said before Emily could answer. "You can use my script when it's your turn to audition."

"But mine was all highlighted and everything."

"I'll highlight your lines in blue when we get to school," Frankie told me. "I'll be yellow, you'll be blue."

"Hey, together you'll make green," Ashley said.

As we started walking towards school, I could feel my mother's hand on my shoulder. I hoped she wasn't going to lecture me. I was already very upset about forgetting my script. And I was nervous about the audition too. The last thing I needed was a lecture.

"I know this is the last thing you need..." my mum began.

Oh no, here it comes.

"But we have to talk about you being better organized, Hank," she continued. "We've gone over this many times."

"I try, Mum. I really do. But every time I think I'm organized, it turns out that I'm not. I don't get it."

"You have to focus," she said. "Your mind is running all over the place."

She was right. I needed to focus. And at that moment, the

thing I needed to concentrate
on was the audition. I made
my brain focus on Aqua Fly.
I forced it to buzz. I imagined
that I was a superhero.
I thought superhero thoughts.

I was so focused I didn't see the patch of ice on the pavement in front of me. I stepped on it and slid about a metre before falling on my butt. One leg headed north, and the other one headed south. My hat flew off and landed in a puddle.

I just sat on the ground, feeling the icy water soaking into the seat of my trousers. And let me tell you this: I had never felt less like a superhero in my whole life.

CHAPTER 6

I spent morning break standing as close as I could to the heater in Head Teacher Love's office. I wasn't in any trouble. It's just that he happens to have the most powerful heater in my school. I didn't care where I was. I just wanted to unfreeze my underpants from my butt. Trust me, it's no fun having icicles in your tighty-whities.

When the bell rang,
I checked my bottom. It was
warm and mostly dry. As
I hurried for the door, Head
Teacher Love tapped me
on the shoulder.

"Your hat, Hank," he said,
handing me my damp blue
knitted hat. "Is there anything
you don't forget?"

"I never forget my birthday,
Mr Love."

"Hank, always remember
these words: being forgetful
puts you on the road to
nowhere."

That didn't make any sense.

"Mr Love, can I ask you a
question? How can there be

a road to nowhere? I mean, isn't nowhere *nowhere*?"

"You'll understand what I'm talking about when you're my age," he said. He licked two fingers and slicked down the single strand of hair on his bald head.

Holy cow. I hope when I'm his age, I have more hair.

I got to class just as the bell rang. Ms Flowers had already

listed everybody's name on
the blackboard. Next to
each name was a blank space
where she would write what
part each person was chosen
to play.

FRANKIE
LUKE
KATIE
ASHLEY
HANK
AVERY
LULA
TOMMY

PEN

"OK, class," Ms Flowers began. "I know you're all nervous. But there's no need to be. Just do the best you can. Let's start with our newest student, Ashley Wong. She was lucky enough to be able to go over the script this weekend with some new friends she made."

Ashley smiled at Frankie and me.

"Everyone say, 'Welcome, Ashley,'" Ms Flowers continued.

We did. Then Ashley walked up to the front of the class, dragging a leg zombie-style behind her. She went right into her babysitter zombie performance.

"Listen, kids," she moaned to three imaginary children. "Don't worry about my eyeball dropping to the ground. I'll pick it up later."

Everyone laughed and applauded. Ashley took a bow and sat down.

"Excellent," Ms Flowers said. "I see we have a little actress among us. What a great way to start off our auditions."

Luke Whitman went next. He set a new low on the disgusting scale when he made a volcano erupt through his nose. Halfway through, Ms Flowers had to send him to the nurse's office for emergency nose repair.

Katie Sperling did a great job playing a pop-up book. Every time she turned a page, she jumped so high her pigtails stood straight up.

But the best of everyone was Frankie playing the part of Barry. He had memorized every line, and there were a lot of them. When he pretended to fall asleep, it was so real you actually thought he was dreaming. I clapped like crazy when he was done. Everyone joined in. We all knew there was no one else that could play Barry.

Then it was my turn.

"Hank, what part have

you chosen to audition for?"
Ms Flowers asked.

"Aqua Fly," I answered.

My heart was thumping as I
walked to the front of the class,
holding Frankie's script. I passed
Ashley's desk.

"You're going to be great,"
she whispered.

It seemed to take for ever
to reach the front of the room.
When I got there, Ms Flowers
had to remind me to turn and
face the class. I took a deep
breath and looked down at the
script. All I saw was a sea of
blue highlights. Those were
the very words I had gone over
all weekend long. And I didn't

recognize one of them.

"Hank, you can start any time you're ready," I heard Ms Flowers say.

I couldn't read. All I could manage to do was buzz. It seemed like I buzzed for twenty minutes. Finally, Ms Flowers interrupted my buzz fest.

"Are you going to say any of the lines?" she asked.

"I am saying the lines," I answered. "I'm just doing it in fly language."

"Interesting," she said. "But I really do need to hear what's written in the script."

I looked at the pages again. Zero. Zippo. Nothing doing.

I had no choice but to buzz to my seat and sit down. The audition was a total flop. My only hope of getting the part was if no one else volunteered.

"Is there anyone else who wants to try out for Aqua Fly?" Ms Flowers asked.

No one answered. That was just what I was hoping for. The part was mine. *Aqua Fly, here I come.*

And then, one single hand popped into the air.

It belonged to Nick McKelty. I had no choice but to make another list in my head.

CHAPTER 7

FIVE THINGS I HOPE WILL HAPPEN TO NICK MCKELTY DURING HIS AUDITION BY HANK ZIPZER

1. His teeth will turn green and start to glow.

2. An alien spaceship will come through the ceiling and take him to their planet until summer.

3. He'll open his mouth to talk and only hiccupy burps will come out.

4. He will actually turn into a fly and buzz right out the window.

5. Oops! I only have time for four. McKelty is about to start.

CHAPTER 8

Unfortunately for me, none of the things on my list happened. What did happen was that McKelty got the part of Aqua Fly. If you ask me, it wasn't because he was so great. It was because, unlike me, he could read the words on the page.

Ms Flowers tried to be nice about it. When everyone was going to lunch, she called me up to her desk.

"I know you tried really hard, Hank," she said. "And for your effort, I have created a special part just for you. One that matches your talents."

That made me feel much better. But what part could that be? Maybe there was going to be a big clock on the library wall, and I would be the bird that popped out every hour and went *cuckoo*. Everyone knows I'm good at sounds.

Or maybe I could be the library cart that gets to roll up and down the aisles. I could attach my bicycle horn and toot it to warn everyone to clear the way for me. That sounded like a lot of fun.

"What is my part, Ms Flowers?"

"Well, Hank, you are going to be a bookmark."

"I *am*? What does a bookmark get to do?"

"First of all, you have to be very quiet. And of course, your most important job will be to hold everyone's places in their books."

"That doesn't sound fun."

"But here's the best part. You'll get to wear the tallest costume of anyone, with two little holes cut out for your eyes. And a red fringe on the bottom to cover your shoes."

OK, I could deal with that. The costume part sounded good. I left the classroom feeling pretty happy about my new role ... until I walked into the lunch room. The first person I saw was McKelty, who was busy shoving tuna casserole into his face right off his tray. He wasn't even using a fork.

"Hey, loser," he said, spraying little bits of fish into the air.

"Too bad I beat you and got the good part."

"That's OK," I said to him.

"I'm going to be a bookmark."

"Ha-ha-ha." He snorted. "Don't you get it? A bookmark doesn't do anything. It just stands there being all bookmark-y."

"Oh yeah?" I answered back. "Ms Flowers said it was a really special part."

"You'll believe anything, Zipperbrain!" Then he added, "See you after lunch in rehearsal. Oh wait, you don't have to be there. You don't have any lines."

"I'll be there," I snapped. "I'm part of the play too."

"Oh, really. Then how come your part isn't even in the script?"

That was a good question. I hadn't thought of that before. Then I realized what had happened. Ms Flowers had made up that part just for me because I can't read very well.

Suddenly, the smell of tuna casserole coming out

of McKelty's mouth made
me feel sick to my stomach.
I ran out into the corridor and
leaned against the wall, trying
so hard not to cry. Before I
knew it, Frankie and Ashley
had left the cafeteria and
were by my side.

"Don't listen to that big
bully," Ashley said. "Bookmarks
are very important. I use one
every day."

"But it's just a tiny part,"
I protested.

"Listen, Hankster," Frankie
said. "No matter what the part
is, you're going to be great."

"Yeah," Ashley chimed in.
"Just wait until rehearsal. You

never know what magic is going
to come spilling out of that
funny head of yours."

Suddenly I was starving, which was a sure sign that I was feeling better. Friends can do that for you.

"OK," I said, heading back into the cafeteria with Frankie and Ashley by my side. "I'm going to be the best bookmark that ever held a place in a book. Look out, world, here comes Hank."

Oh, and by the way, about the tuna casserole: if you ever see even a glop of it on your plate, change plates. I didn't, and my tongue is still not talking to me.

CHAPTER 9

After lunch, we went back to
class. Ms Flowers had moved all
the desks into a wide semicircle,
so we had the entire centre of
the room to rehearse our play.

"Let's have all the people
playing books stand on the
left," she said, "and everyone
else on the right."

I followed her directions.

"No, Hank," Ms Flowers said.
"You're supposed to be on the
right."

"I know," I answered.
"That's where I am."

"Hank, you are on the left side," she explained. "Do you know which way is left and which is right?"

"I always guess, and every now and then I'm right."

"Well, not this time, Zipperfang," McKelty said with a snort. "Only a birdbrain doesn't know right from left."

"You better not ruffle the feathers of this bird, McKelty!" I shot back.

Everyone laughed, and I felt pretty good about that. The score: Hank Zipzer, one. Nick McKelty, zero.

Ms Flowers led me to my place. Then Frankie sat down at a table she had put in the centre of the circle.

"You may begin reading your lines," she said to him. "Remember that you are alone in the library, and it's late at night."

Frankie yawned and stretched.

"'The library is so dark and quiet when everyone is gone,'" he read. "'It feels like a magical place where anything could happen.'"

He put his head down on the table and pretended to fall asleep.

"'I wonder if I'll dream about books,'" he muttered, just before he closed his eyes.

"Excellent," Ms Flowers said. "Remember to say your lines loud enough so everyone can hear you. And now, all the children who are playing books start to come alive. Think about the title of your book, and then come up with the way you would move."

Instantly, Ashley went into her zombie walk. McKelty flapped his arms and started to buzz like Aqua Fly. Luke threw his arms over his head and pretended he was an erupting volcano. I was standing next

to Luke, and let me tell you,
this volcano never showered.
When his arms went over his
head, his armpits smelled like
rotten bananas.

My nose started to twitch. The hairs inside felt like they were curling up into little hair balls. Without even thinking, I moved away from him and found myself in the middle of the circle.

"Hank," Ms Flowers said. "You're playing a bookmark. You're supposed to be *in* the books, not in front of them."

"But I'm a bookmark with a lot of personality," I said.

Everyone laughed again, so I started to think about what a bookmark with a lot of personality would do. He wouldn't just sit between the pages of a book. Maybe he would wiggle his way to another page. You know, like a worm crawling around on the ground.

As soon as that thought popped into my brain, I dropped to the floor. My body was off and wiggling across the stage area.

"What are you doing, Hank?" Ms Flowers said with a smile. I guess she had never seen a bookmark flopping across her classroom before.

"I am looking for my place in the best book," I said.

"Well then, wiggle on over to me," Ashley said. "Zombies are always fun to read about."

I twisted and squirmed and rolled all the way over to Ashley. Everybody in the class was cracking up. Even Ms Flowers couldn't stop herself from laughing.

"You're not going to put that stupid wiggling junk in the play, are you?" McKelty grumbled. His face was as red as a radish.

"Are you kidding?" Frankie said to him. "Hank is being really funny."

"But he's not supposed to be funny," McKelty answered. "Besides, the parents are here to see *me* in the play. *I'm* the star."

There he was, being Nick McKelty again. He never tells the truth. It's always the truth times one hundred. Frankie and I call that the McKelty Factor. Ashley didn't know about the McKelty Factor. But when she heard it in action, she went nuts.

"You are so not the star of the play," she said to him. "Every one of us is important. And remember, you're a fly. Everyone wants to swat you."

We all cracked up at that. Boy, oh, boy, did that ever make McKelty mad. He frowned so hard his lips almost dropped to the floor.

"OK, everyone,"
Ms Flowers said, trying to
settle us all down. "We have
a lot of work to do. The play
is only two days away."

"So can I keep the wiggle
in?" I asked her.

"Only if you keep it very
short," she said. "Remember,
a little wiggle goes a long
way."

We went on with the
rehearsal, but McKelty kept
giving me angry looks. Once,
when I was standing next
to him, he leaned over and
whispered in my ear.

"You better not try to steal
the show again, Zippernose,"

he said, snarling at me through his slimy green teeth. It looked like there was a bunch of lettuce growing in there.

"What are you going to do about it?" I snarled back.

"Let's just say, you'll be sorry."

I gulped hard. As much as I don't like to admit it, that Nick McKelty can be very scary.

CHAPTER 10

All the next day, we rehearsed
very hard. The best part about
it was that we got to skip
maths and spelling. Any day
I can skip maths is a good day
for my brain. And not having
to take a spelling test is like
a mini holiday. By the end
of school, everyone seemed
ready.

Since I didn't have any
lines, my rehearsal time was
shorter than everyone else's.

So Ms Flowers had me work on
my bookmark costume. I stapled
lots of sheets of card together,
and then cut a fringe at the
top and the bottom. To make
it look really cool, I took a
black crayon and wrote the
word BOKMARK right down
the middle.

"Hey, Zip," Frankie whispered
to me on one of his breaks.
"Hand me that black crayon."

"How come?"

"You left out one of the *O*s in
book," he said. "It has two *O*s."

I handed him the crayon, and
he added a very skinny *O* to
make it look like it had always
been there.

I'm so lucky to have a friend
like Frankie. He always saves me
from being really embarrassed.

The next day was the big
performance. All our mums and
dads were coming to see us.

We were so excited. Everyone
got there early. We helped
Ms Flowers arrange the chairs
for the parents around the
edge of the classroom. Lots
of us brought snacks for the
treat table. Frankie's mum made

her famous brownies without walnuts, in case any kids were allergic to nuts. Katie Sperling brought rice-crispy treats that she decorated with M&M's.

My mum, of course, had to be different. She sent in a deli tray with nothing on it that even looked like food. Well, there was one thing that could have been tuna fish, but nobody was willing to taste it and find out for sure.

Ms Flowers had us wait in the corridor while the parents filed in and took their seats. Once they were in the room, we put on our costumes. Frankie just wore a jumper and jeans. Ashley had a zombie wig with fake blood dripping off it. The top of my costume went up over my face, so I had to cut out holes for my eyes and mouth.

Just before the play was about to start, Ms Flowers came out into the corridor to check our costumes and give us a pep talk.

"Is everyone ready?" she asked.

"Everyone but Nick McKelty," Ashley answered. "He went to the toilet."

"I always wee a lot when I'm nervous too," Luke Whitman said. "Before my oral report on Thomas Edison, I must have gone to the toilet twenty times."

"That's something we really don't need to know," Katie Sperling said.

"As soon as Nick returns, I'll introduce you," Ms Flowers said. "There's no reason to be nervous. You all know your lines. If you just concentrate and work together, nothing will go wrong."

Just then, Nick McKelty ran down the corridor. Well, he was half running and half hopping, trying to tie his Aqua Fly wings back on.

"Are you ready, Nick?" Ms Flowers asked.

"You should have heard me practising in the toilet," he bragged. "I smashed it."

"How do you know?" I said to him. "Did all the sinks applaud?"

"That's so funny I forgot to laugh," he snarled.

"That's enough, boys," Ms Flowers said. "Remember,

keep your mind on the play
and enjoy yourselves."

She went into the classroom.

"Welcome to Children's
Reading Week," we heard
Ms Flowers say to the parents.
"And now, allow me to present
the Room Four Players, starring
in *A Night at the Library*."

The parents clapped as
we all filed in and took our
places.

I looked out and saw a sea
of flashing lights, some from
real cameras and some from
mobile phones. My mum and
dad were there, and so was
Papa Pete. It was easy to
pick him out because he was

wearing his favourite bright
red tracksuit. It makes him look
like a ripe strawberry.

The parents went very quiet, and then Frankie began. And once he fell asleep, the "books" came alive. It was all going great. Katie popped up. Luke erupted. And the parents were laughing their heads off.

Then it was Nick McKelty's turn. He buzzed right by me and introduced himself to the audience, adding buzzing sounds in between the words.

"Say hello ... *buzz* ... to Aqua Fly ... *buzz* ... the most powerful ... superhero ... that ever landed on a tomato ... *buzz*."

The parents laughed, and McKelty seemed pretty pleased with himself.

Then it was my turn.
I stepped out and dropped
to the floor. I wiggled over to
Ashley, being careful not
to over-wiggle. Ashley flashed
me a smile. When I saw that,
it tickled my brain. Suddenly,
from nowhere, my mouth flew
open and in my best bookmark
voice, out came these words:

"I am here to hold your place
and put a big smile on your
face."

I heard the parents laugh.
A few even clapped. I felt great.
I rose to my feet, being careful
not to trip on my fringe.
I turned to face my family,
so they would get a good

picture of me. As I took a step,
I felt something under my foot.
It was a shoe — a big shoe —
that could only belong to Nick
McKelty. He had stuck his foot
out in front of me, and since

I couldn't look down in my costume, I tripped over it.

"Let me know what the floor looks like," McKelty whispered with a nasty laugh. "I told you what would happen if you tried to steal my show." That was the last thing I heard before I fell.

As I was going down, I knew there was nothing I could do to stop it. I was going to make a fool of myself in front of everyone.

Then it came to me. A line, a really funny line, just popped into my head.

"Oops," I said, as I hit the floor. "I lost my *plaaaaaaaaaaaace*."

The audience laughed, thinking it was part of the play. But I didn't laugh. My purple costume ripped right in two, and I thought I might have split my trousers. I was too scared to look.

The only thing I saw for sure was McKelty's face, laughing down at me.

"Remember, Zippercreep," he said. "I'm the star. Not you!"

And at that moment, lying there on the floor, I totally believed him.

CHAPTER 11

I was sprawled out on the
floor, my costume destroyed,
my trousers probably ripped.

I didn't know what to do.
But Ms Flowers had told us
that an important rule in plays
is that "the show must go on".
No matter what, you have to
keep the show going.

So I figured that the best
thing for me to do was to get
out of the middle of the stage
so the play could go on. I pulled

myself along the floor until I reached Ashley, who held out a hand and dragged me the rest of the way.

This made Nick McKelty even angrier, because the parents weren't watching him, they were watching me. And let me say, this was one time I didn't want to be the centre of attention.

"Carry on, kids," Ms Flowers whispered. "You know what comes next."

Frankie lifted his head off the desk and pretended to wake up. He yawned and stretched.

"I had the strangest dream," he said. "The books were alive."

Everyone stood very still, except Nick McKelty.

This was the part of the play where Aqua Fly was supposed to buzz over to Frankie and tell him it was not a dream at all. That books always come alive, as long as we believe in them. Ms Flowers had told us it was the biggest moment of the play. It was the line she was most proud of writing.

McKelty buzzed over and took his place next to Frankie.

He opened his mouth, but all that came out was a buzzing sound. That would have been OK, but the next thing that came out of his mouth was another buzzing sound. And then another one. And another one.

"Say your lines, Nick," Frankie whispered. "We have to finish the play."

"Buzz," Nick said. *"Buzz, buzz, buzz!"*

There was panic in his eyes.

"You can't just buzz," Frankie told him.

"Buzz," McKelty answered.

"No, say the words!" Frankie whispered.

"I forgot them," McKelty whispered back. I could see his hands starting to shake with fear. He looked like Katherine, the iguana, the first time she saw Papa Pete's cat, Morris.

I looked around and saw
everyone in the audience waiting
for the big ending. Ms Flowers
was trying to mouth the words
to McKelty, but he wouldn't
look at her. He just stood there,
buzzing.

Without even thinking about it,
I jumped to my feet and shuffled

my way over to Frankie.
He looked just as surprised
as I was. When I opened my
mouth, I couldn't believe what
came out.

"I am just a lowly bookmark,"
I said. "But one thing I know for
sure: books always come alive
when we believe in them."

"So this wasn't a dream?"
Frankie said.

"No," I answered. "Not at
all. All the books here are alive
and waiting for you whenever
you want to have a great
adventure."

And without thinking, Frankie
and I threw our arms around
each other.

The parents started to
applaud.

"Thanks for coming," I said
to the parents. "The Room Four
Players have enjoyed putting on
this play for you."

All the kids came forward to
take a bow. Everyone but Nick
McKelty. He was still buzzing.

After the play, we all got
behind the treat table and
served our parents lemonade
and snacks. Luke Whitman was
the only one who ate my mum's
so-called deli meats. But that
wasn't surprising, since he also
enjoys already-chewed gum he
finds in his pockets.

"Hankie, my boy," Papa Pete
said, as I put a rice-crispy treat
on his plate. "You were so
great. It looked like you saved
the day."

"Yes," my mum chimed in.
"We thought you didn't have
any lines in the play."

"Well," I said. "That's what
was supposed to happen. But

when McKelty froze up, I had to jump in."

"But how did you know the lines?" Papa Pete asked.

"I have a good memory," I said. "I learned everyone's lines by hearing them over and over while we were rehearsing."

"Such a smart boy." Papa Pete beamed.

That made me feel very happy. I always think Emily is the smart one in our family, not me.

I really loved it when all the kids and Ms Flowers thanked me for saving the play. The only one who didn't congratulate me

was — you guessed it — Nick
McKelty.

"I could have done those
lines better than
you," he said,
shoving his third
brownie in his
mouth.
"Yeah?
Well, why
didn't you?"
"I wasn't in the mood."
As for me, I was in a really
good mood. Even Nick McKelty
couldn't make me feel bad. I
was on top of the world. I felt
great. So great that I just had
to make a list.